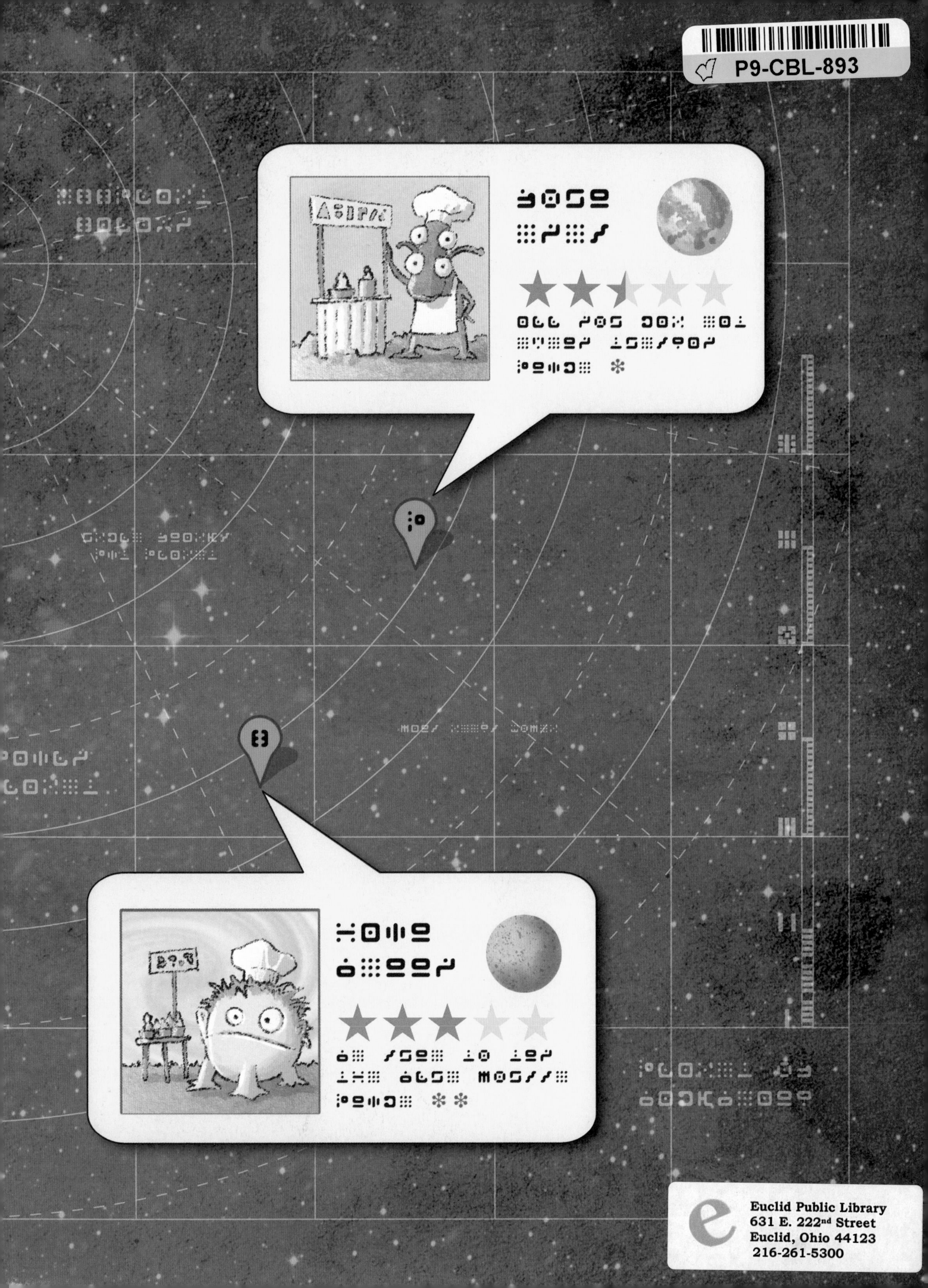

EVEN ALIENS NEED SNACKS

Matthew McElligott

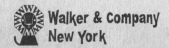 Walker & Company
New York

To Christy, Anthony, Mom, Pop, and Gingie "Knuckles" Nice

First published in the United States of America in August 2012
by Walker Publishing Company, Inc., a division of Bloomsbury Publishing, Inc.
www.bloomsburykids.com

For information about permission to reproduce selections from this book, write to
Permissions, Walker BFYR, 175 Fifth Avenue, New York, New York 10010

Library of Congress Cataloging-in-Publication data
McElligott, Matthew.
Even aliens need snacks / Matthew McElligott.
p.   cm.
Summary: Creating snacks that make most humans queasy,
a young chef finds a new clientele—aliens.
ISBN 978-0-8027-2398-7 (hardcover) • ISBN 978-0-8027-2399-4 (reinforced)
[1. Cooking—Fiction. 2. Extraterrestrial beings—Fiction. 3. Humorous stories.] I. Title.
PZ7.M478448Et 2012   [E]—dc23   2011050071

Illustrations created with ink, pencil, and digital techniques
Typeset in Aunt Mildred
Book design by Nicole Gastonguay

Printed in China by Hung Hing Printing (China) Co., Ltd., Shenzhen, Guangdong
2 4 6 8 10 9 7 5 3 1 (hardcover)
2 4 6 8 10 9 7 5 3 1 (reinforced)

All papers used by Bloomsbury Publishing, Inc., are natural, recyclable products
made from wood grown in well-managed forests. The manufacturing processes
conform to the environmental regulations of the country of origin.

My mom is a great cook.
She always lets me help out
in the kitchen.

She even lets me make up my own recipes. Today I invented an eggplant, mustard, and lemonade smoothie. It's delicious.

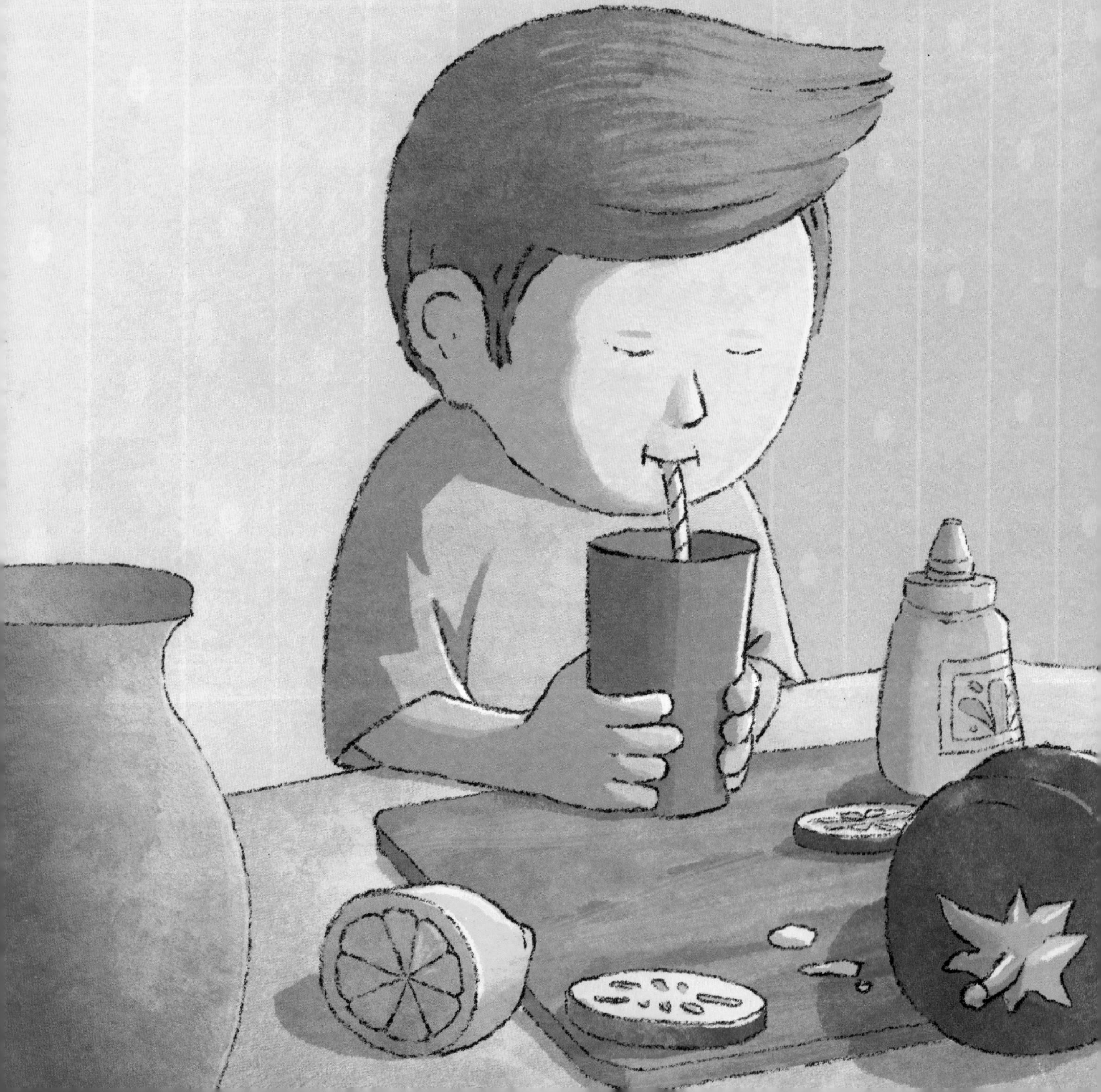

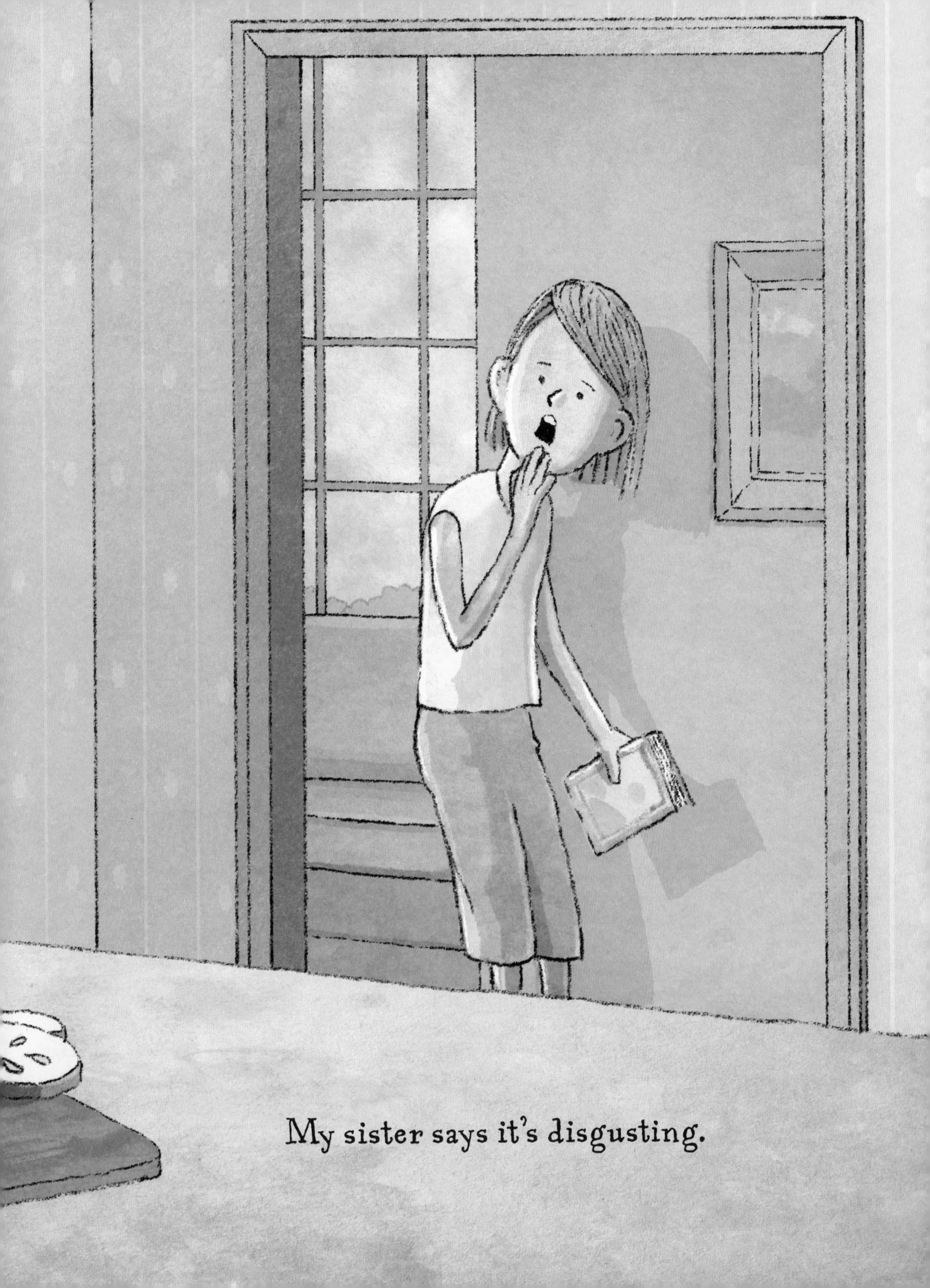

My sister says it's disgusting.

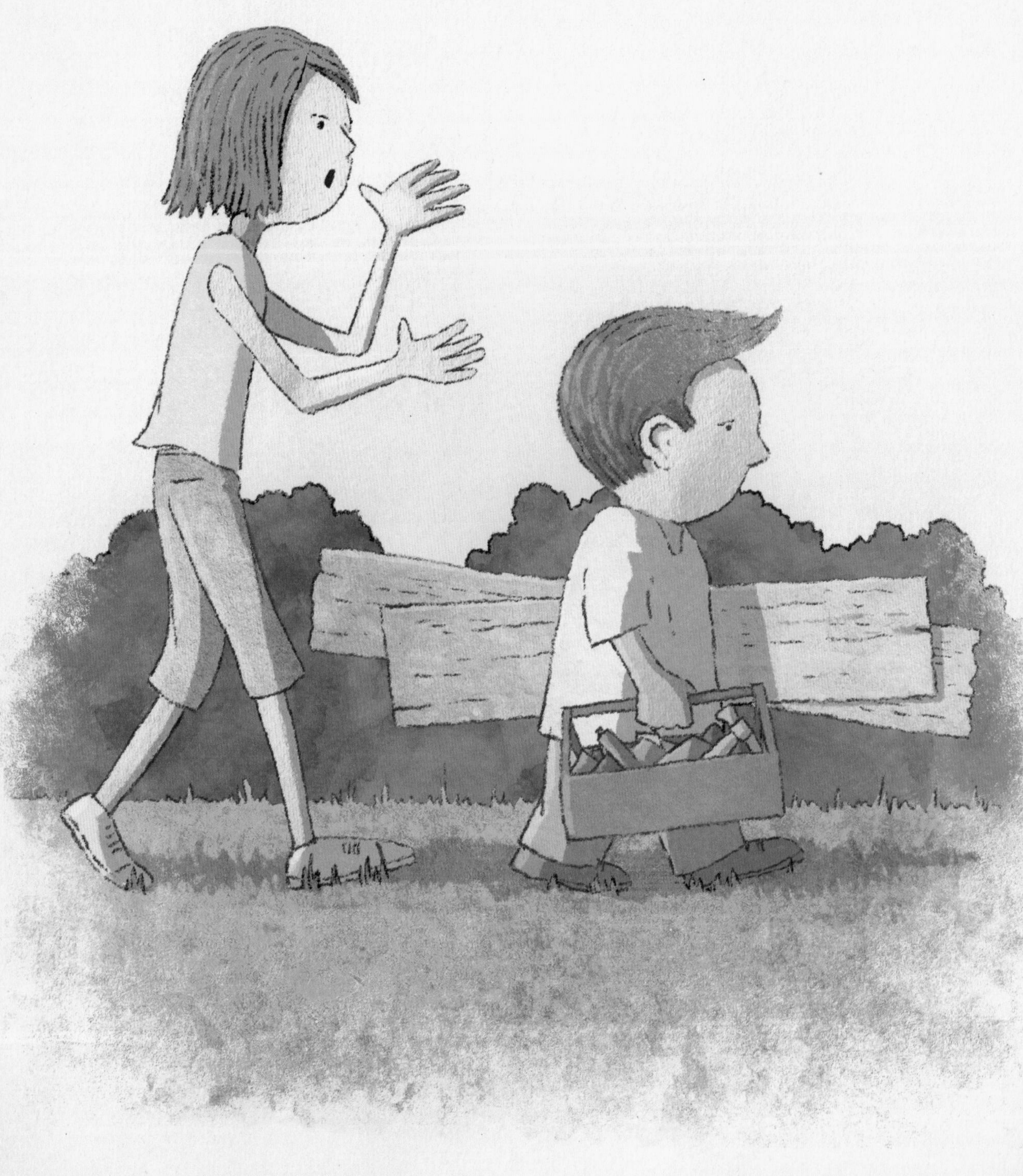

She says that no one in the world
would eat the things I cook.

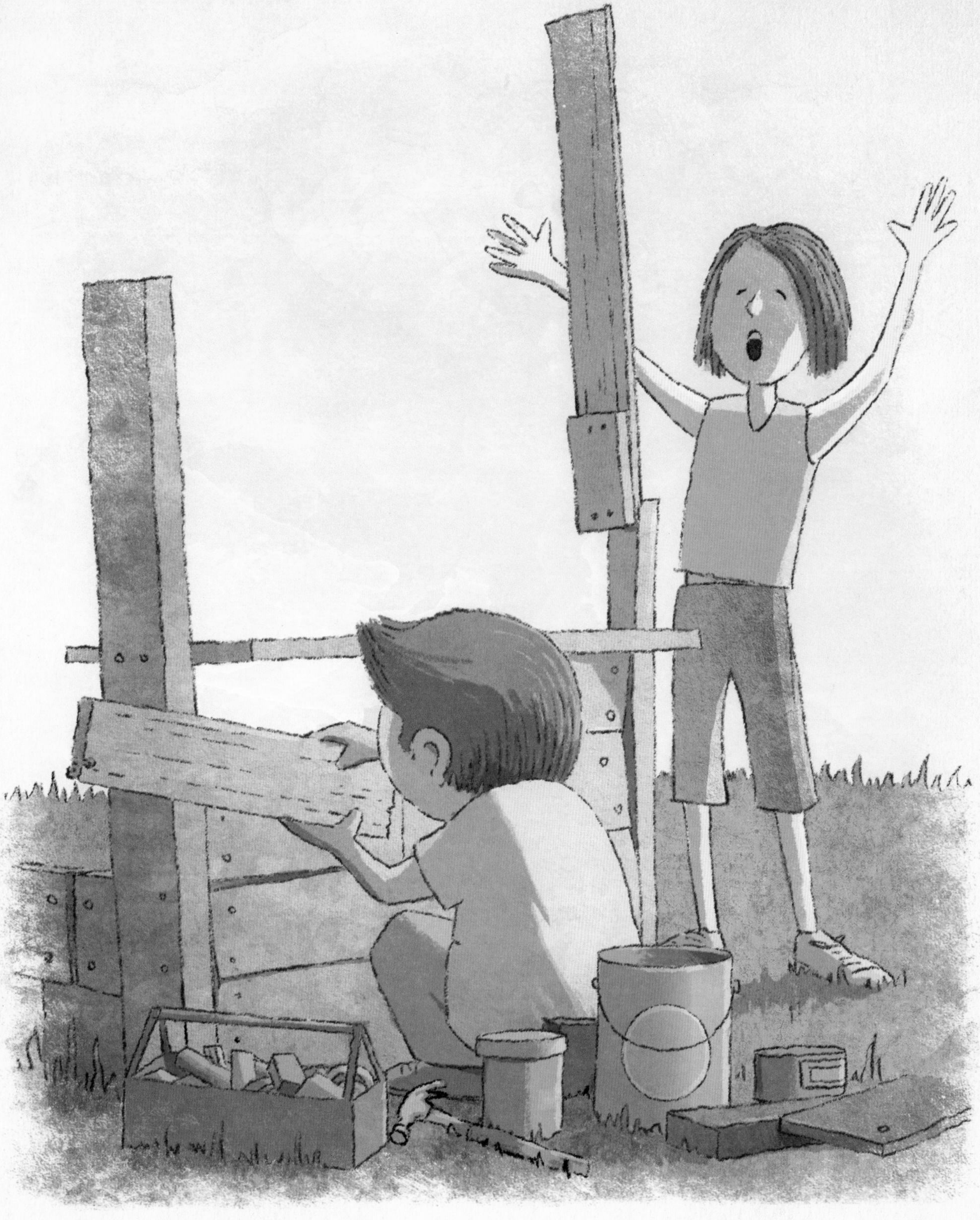

She says that no one in the whole
universe would eat the things I cook.

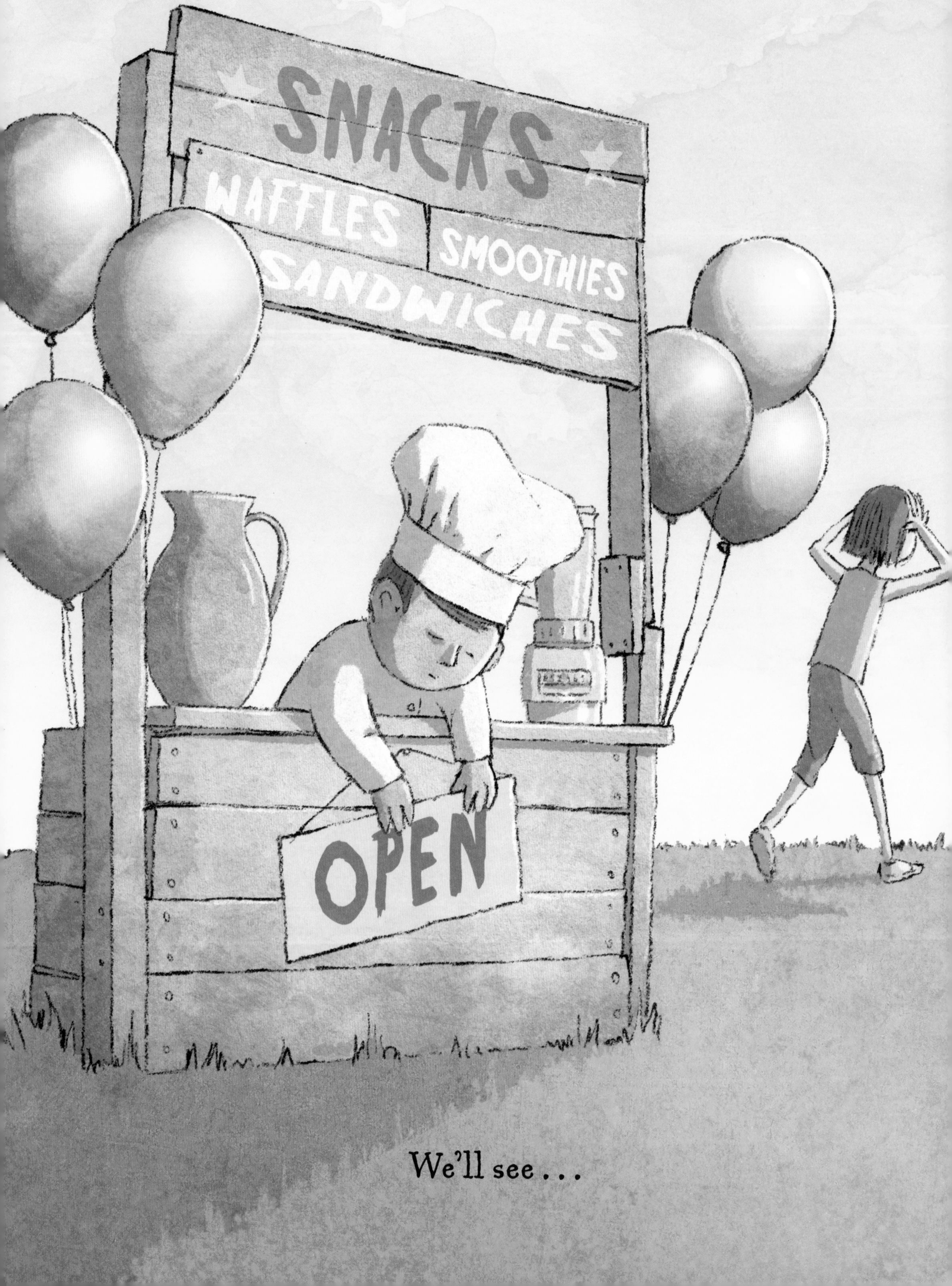
SNACKS
WAFFLES
SMOOTHIES
SANDWICHES
OPEN

We'll see . . .

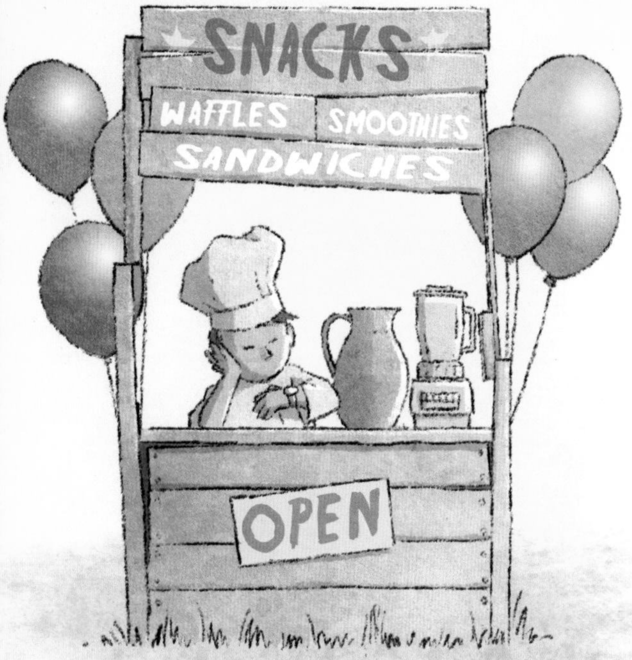
SNACKS
WAFFLES
SMOOTHIES
SANDWICHES
OPEN

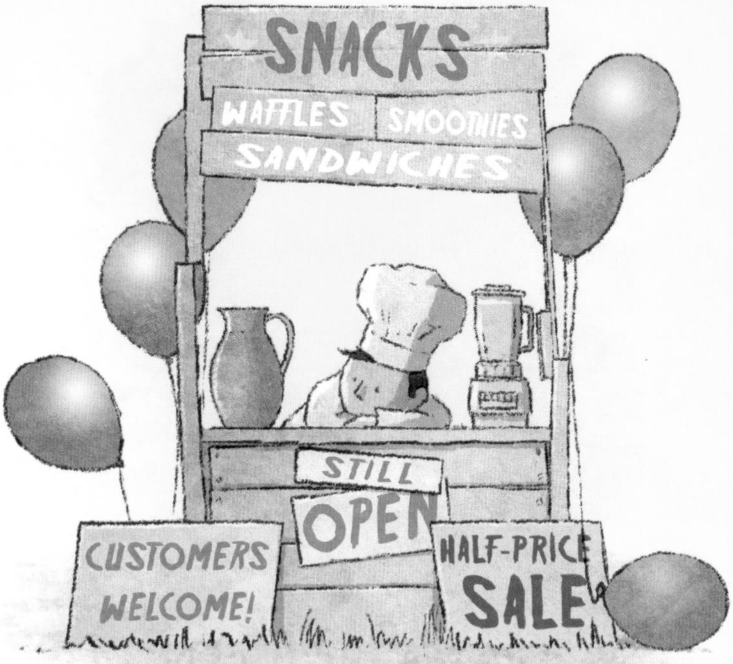
SNACKS
WAFFLES
SMOOTHIES
SANDWICHES
STILL
OPEN
CUSTOMERS WELCOME!
HALF-PRICE SALE

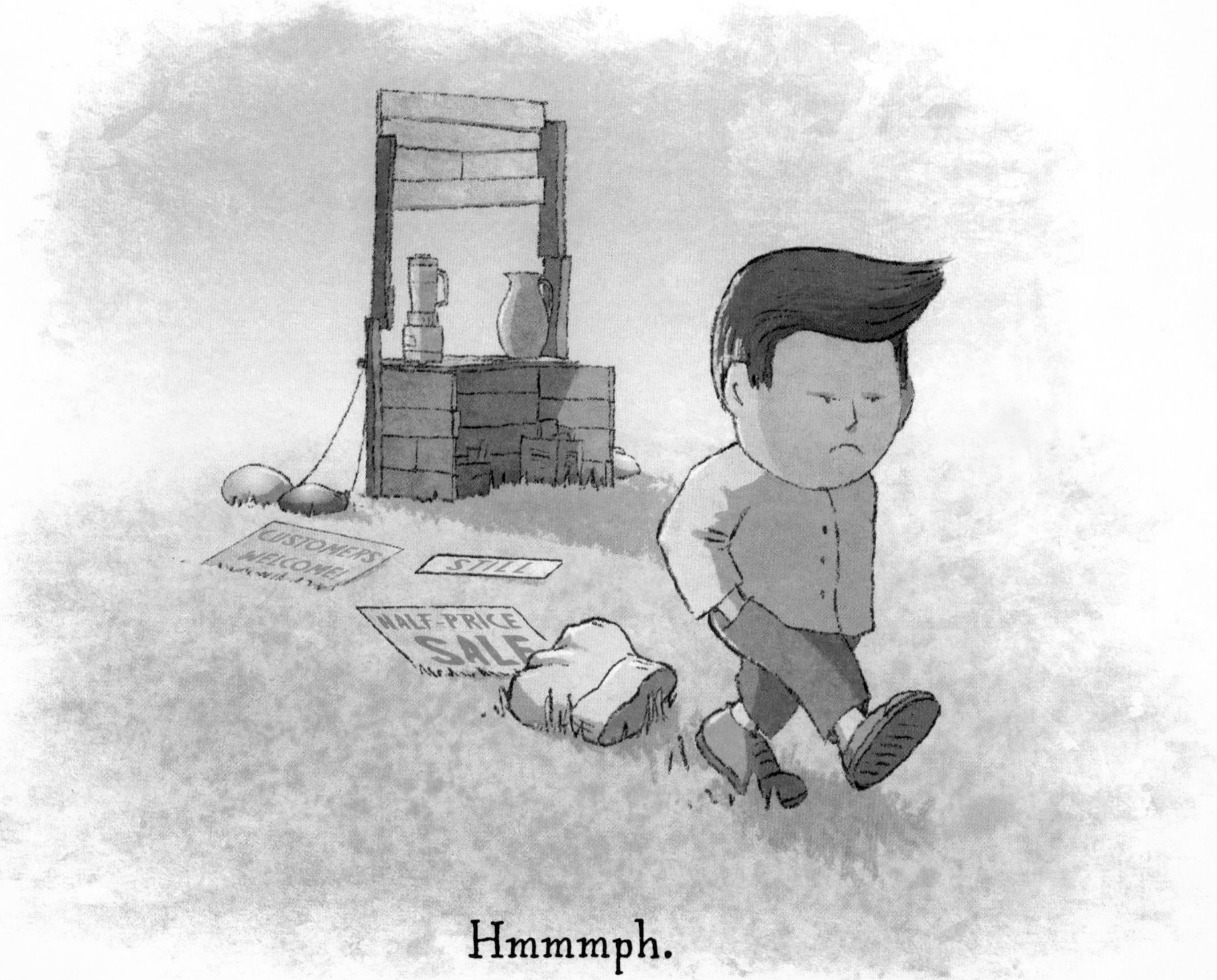
CUSTOMERS WELCOME!
STILL
HALF-PRICE SALE

Hmmmph.

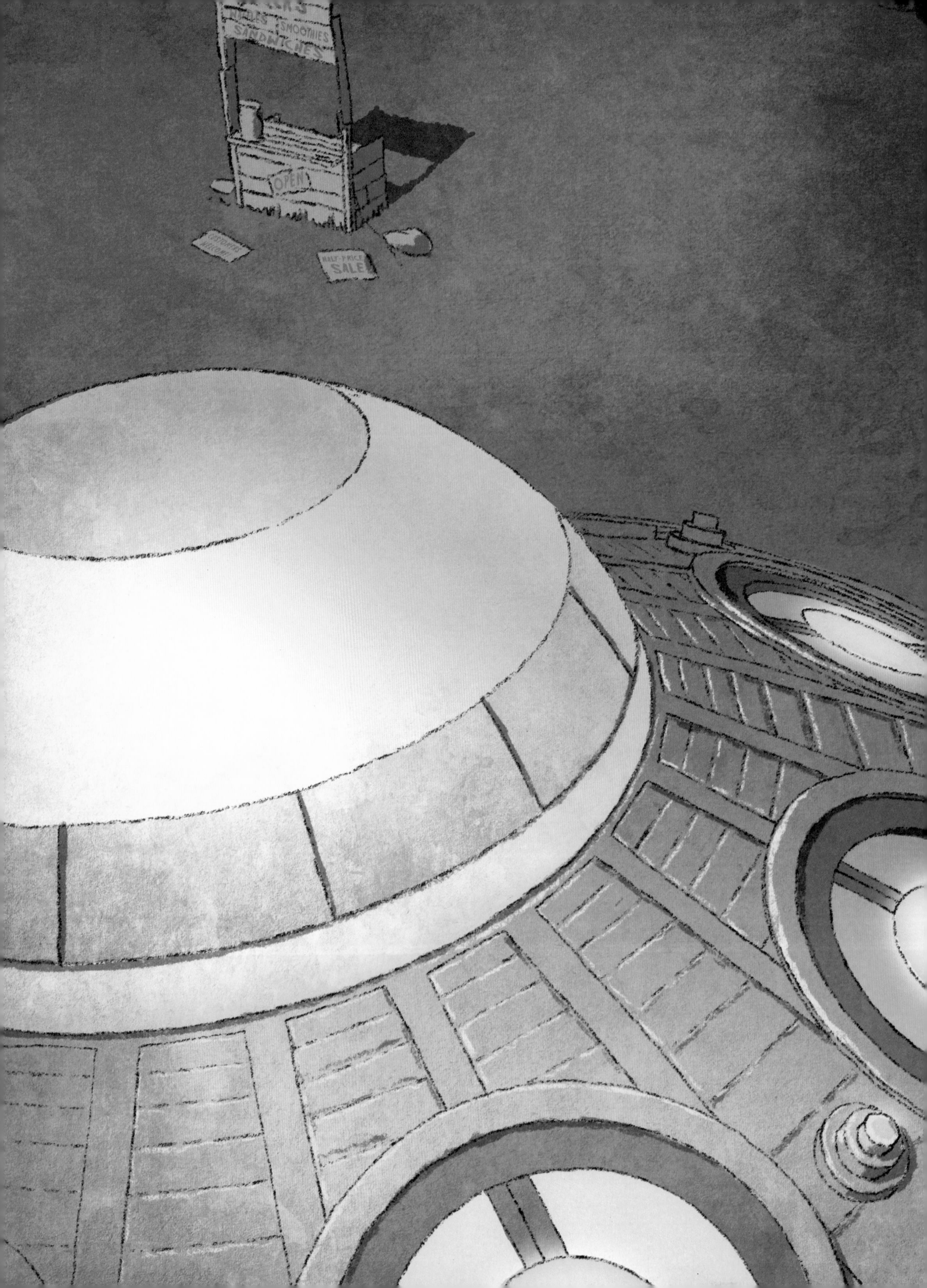
SMOOTHIES
SANDWICHES
OPEN
HALF-PRICE SALE

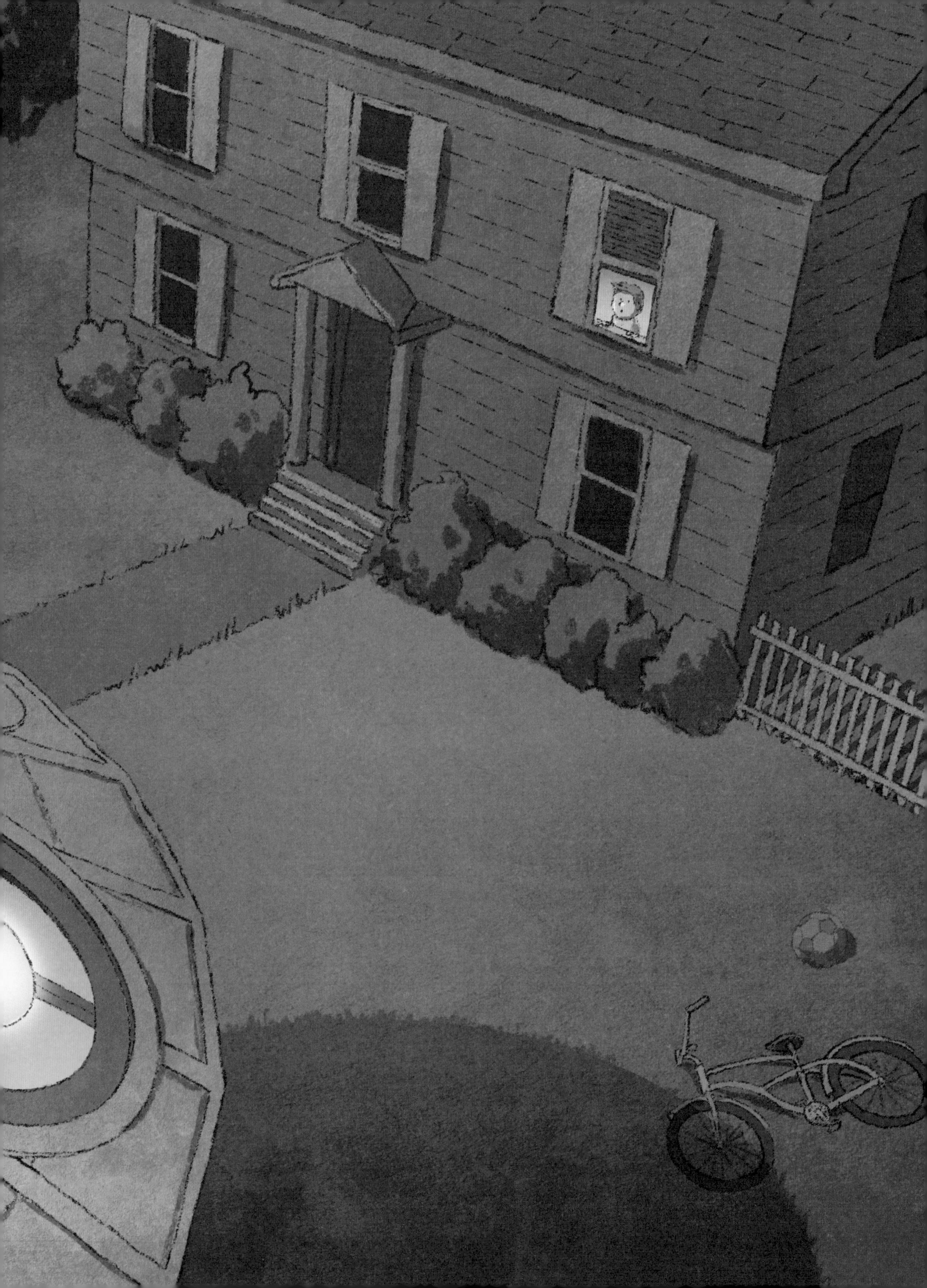

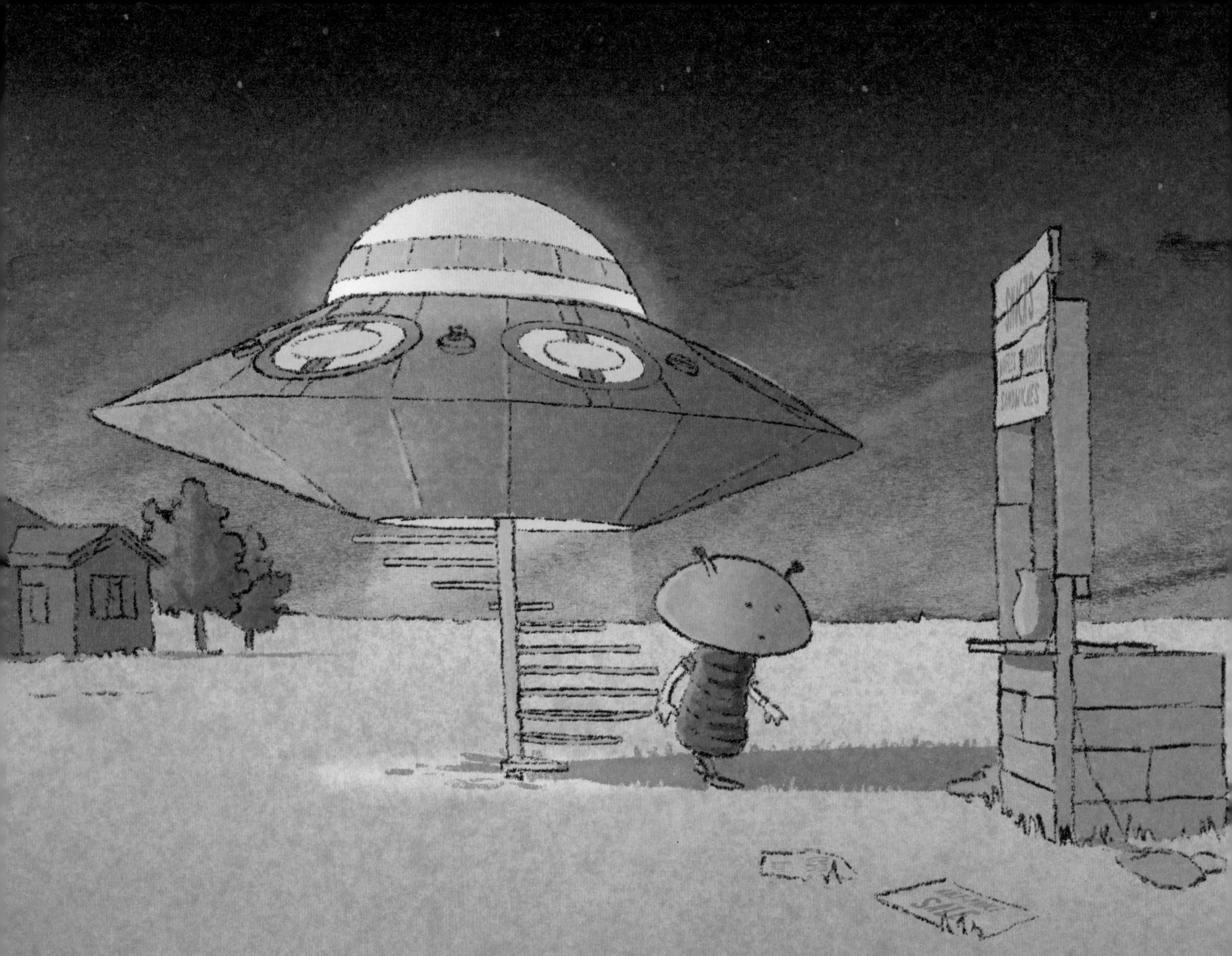

I knew my idea was good! I just had the hours wrong.

I run back inside and get dressed.

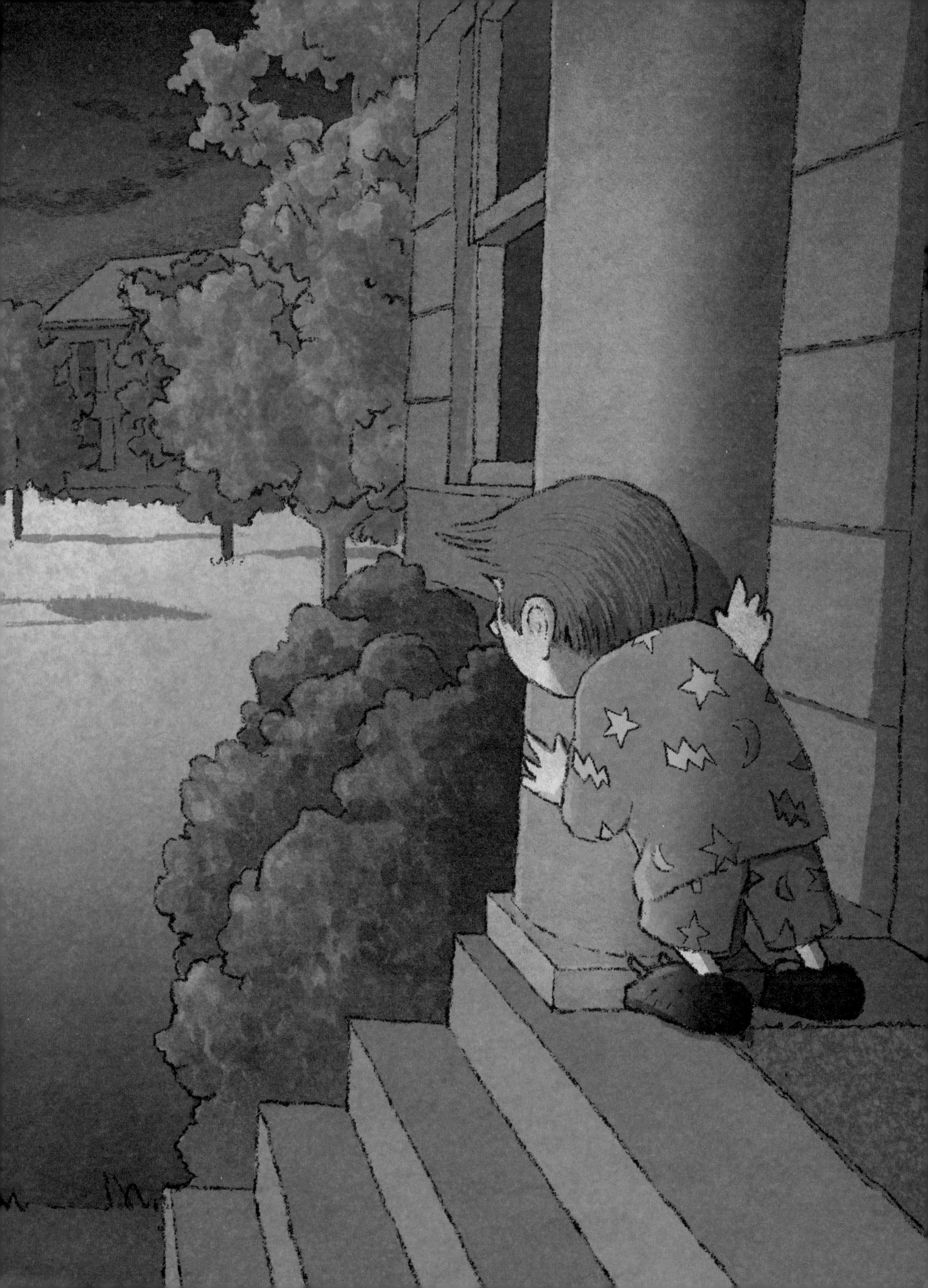

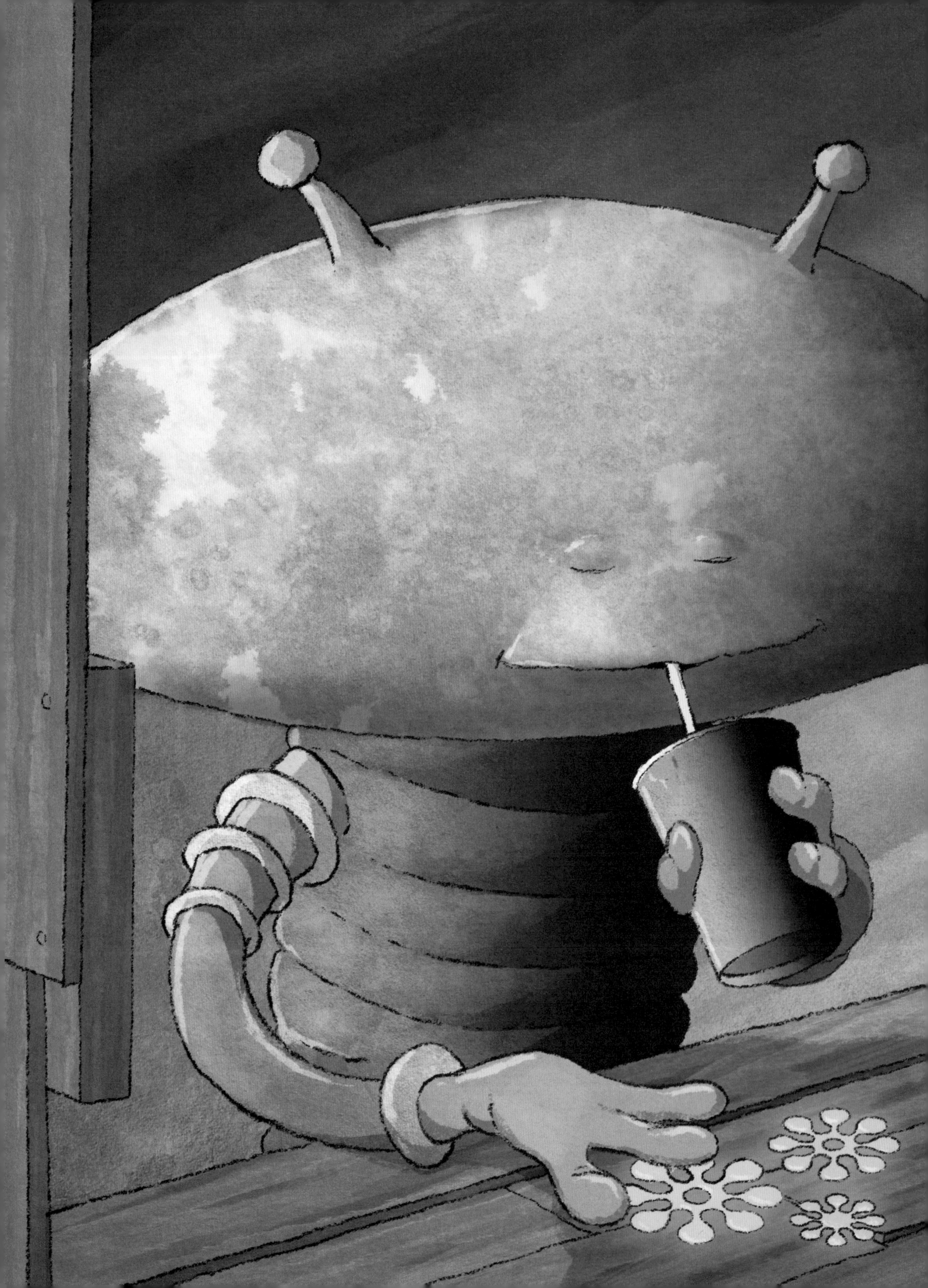

My first customer is from out of town.

He really likes my mushroom iced tea. I think he even tries to pay me for it.

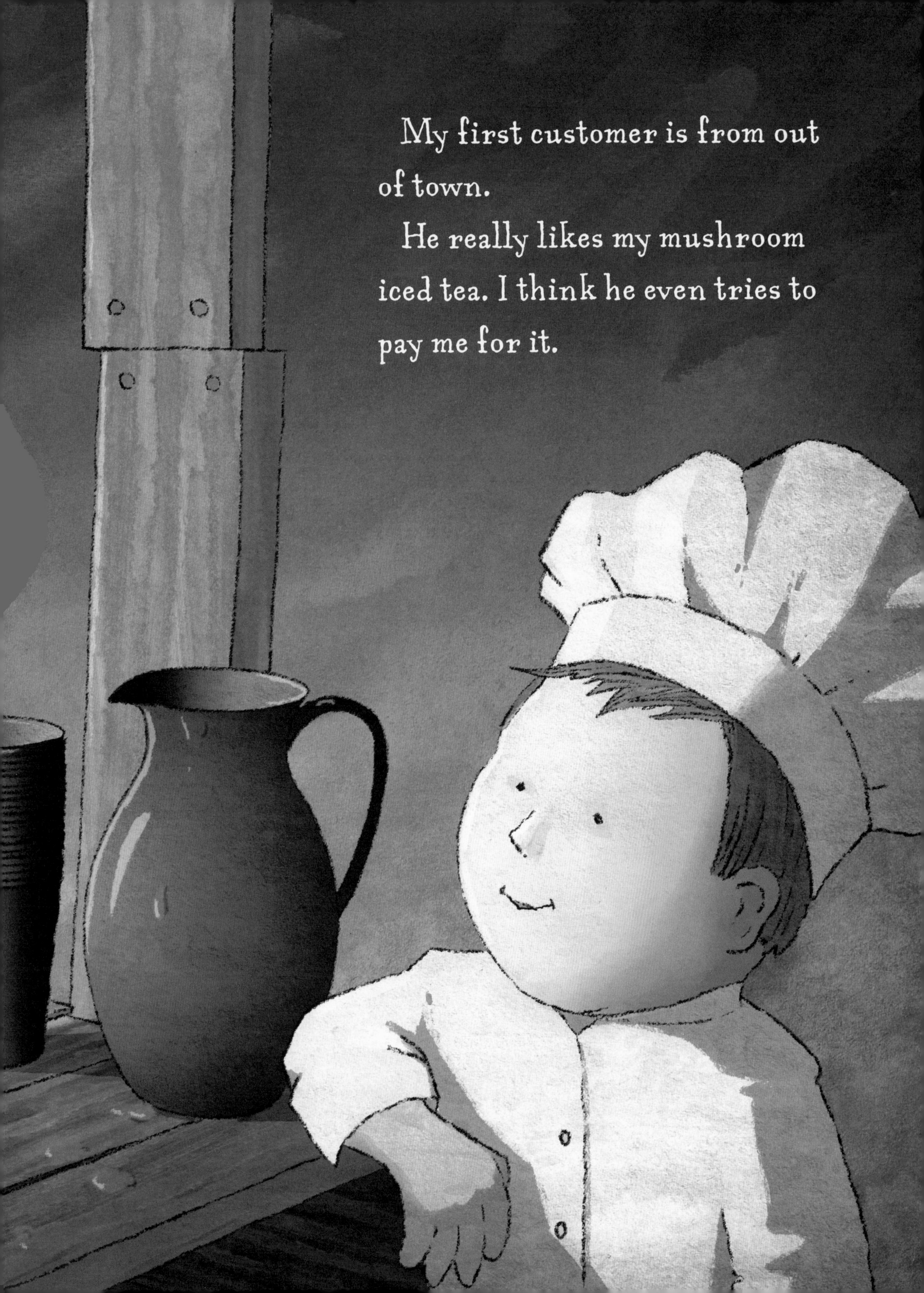

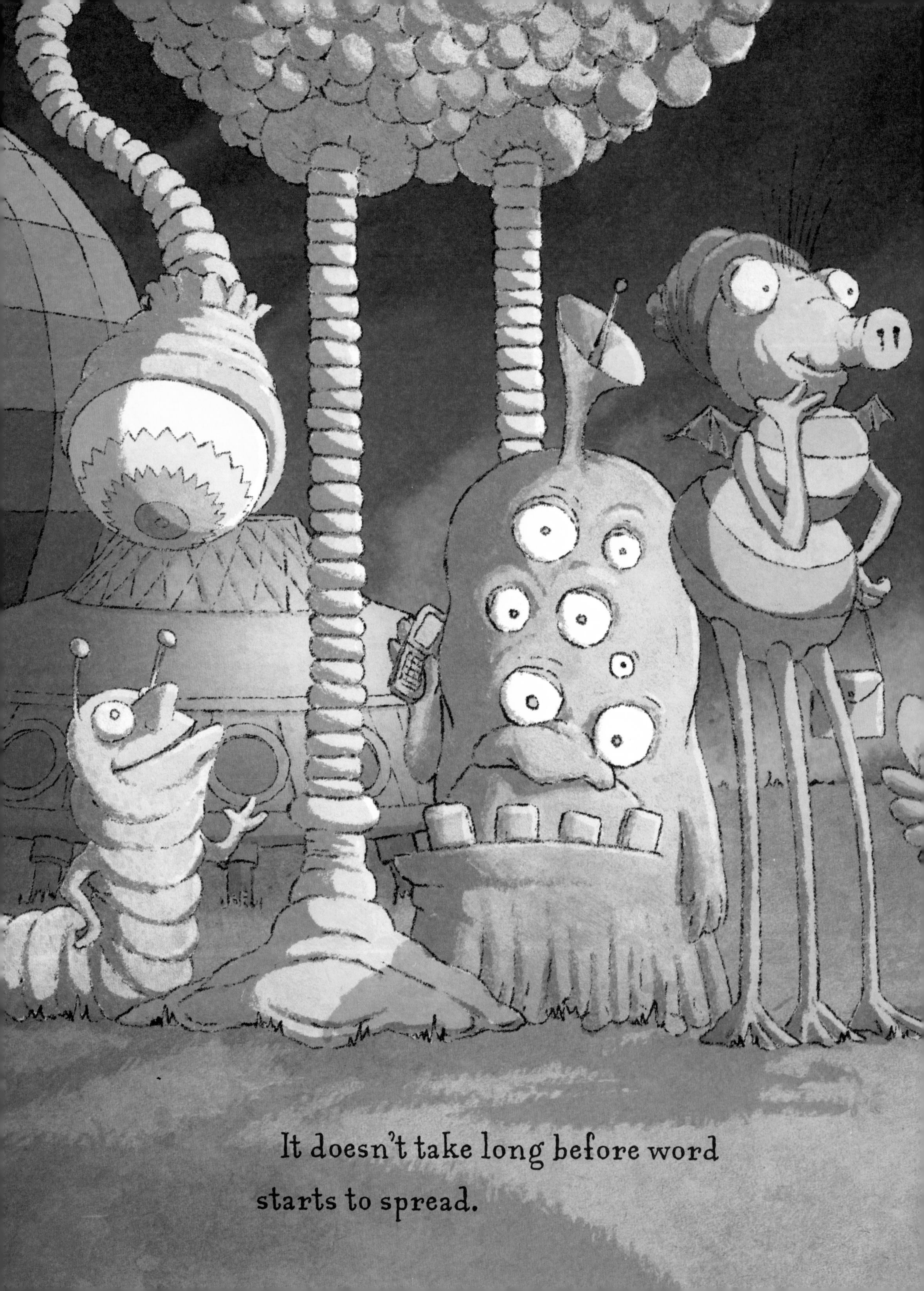

It doesn't take long before word
starts to spread.

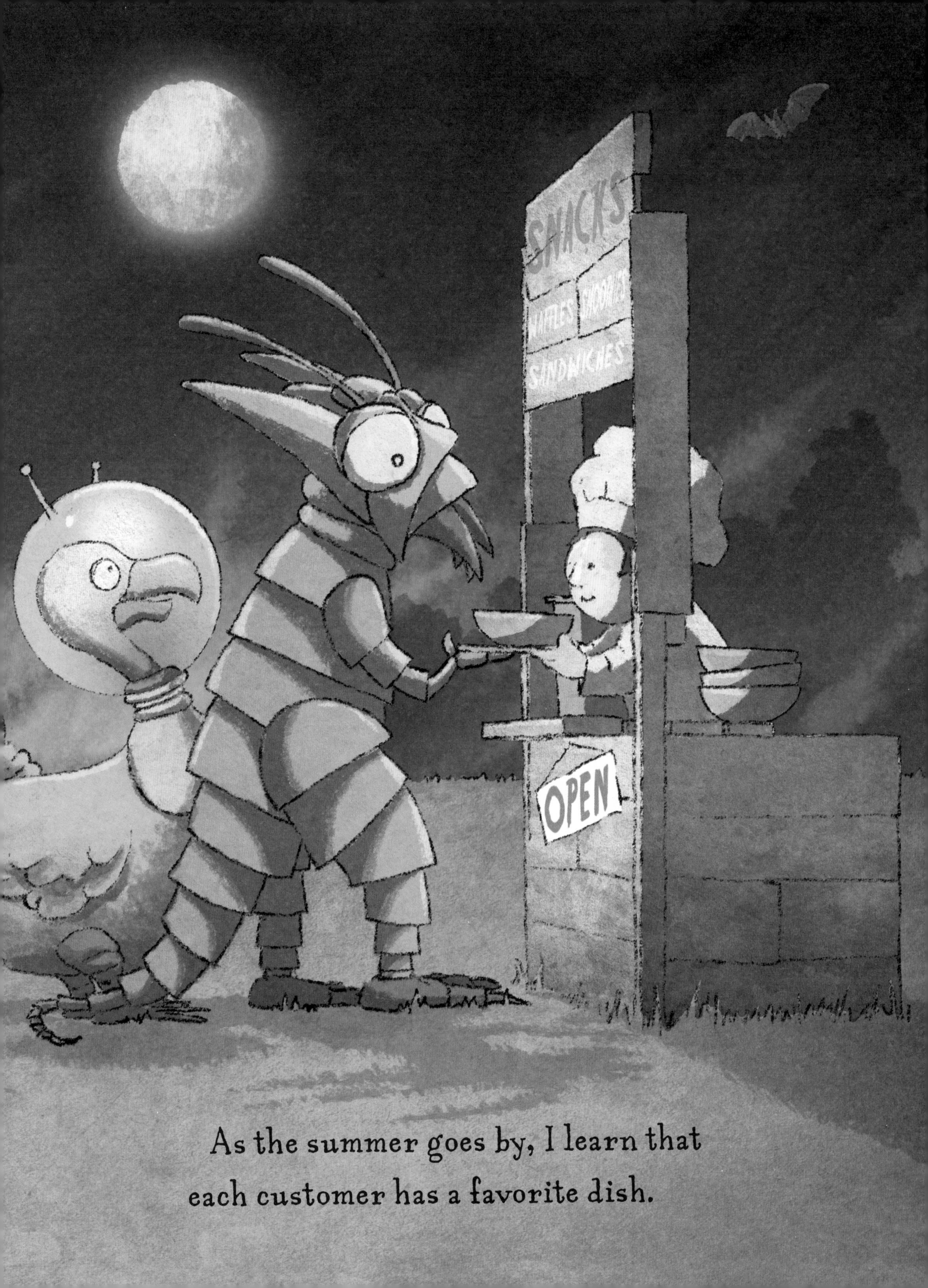
SNACKS
WAFFLES
SMOOTHIES
SANDWICHES
OPEN

As the summer goes by, I learn that each customer has a favorite dish.

Some like my Swiss cheese donut holes.

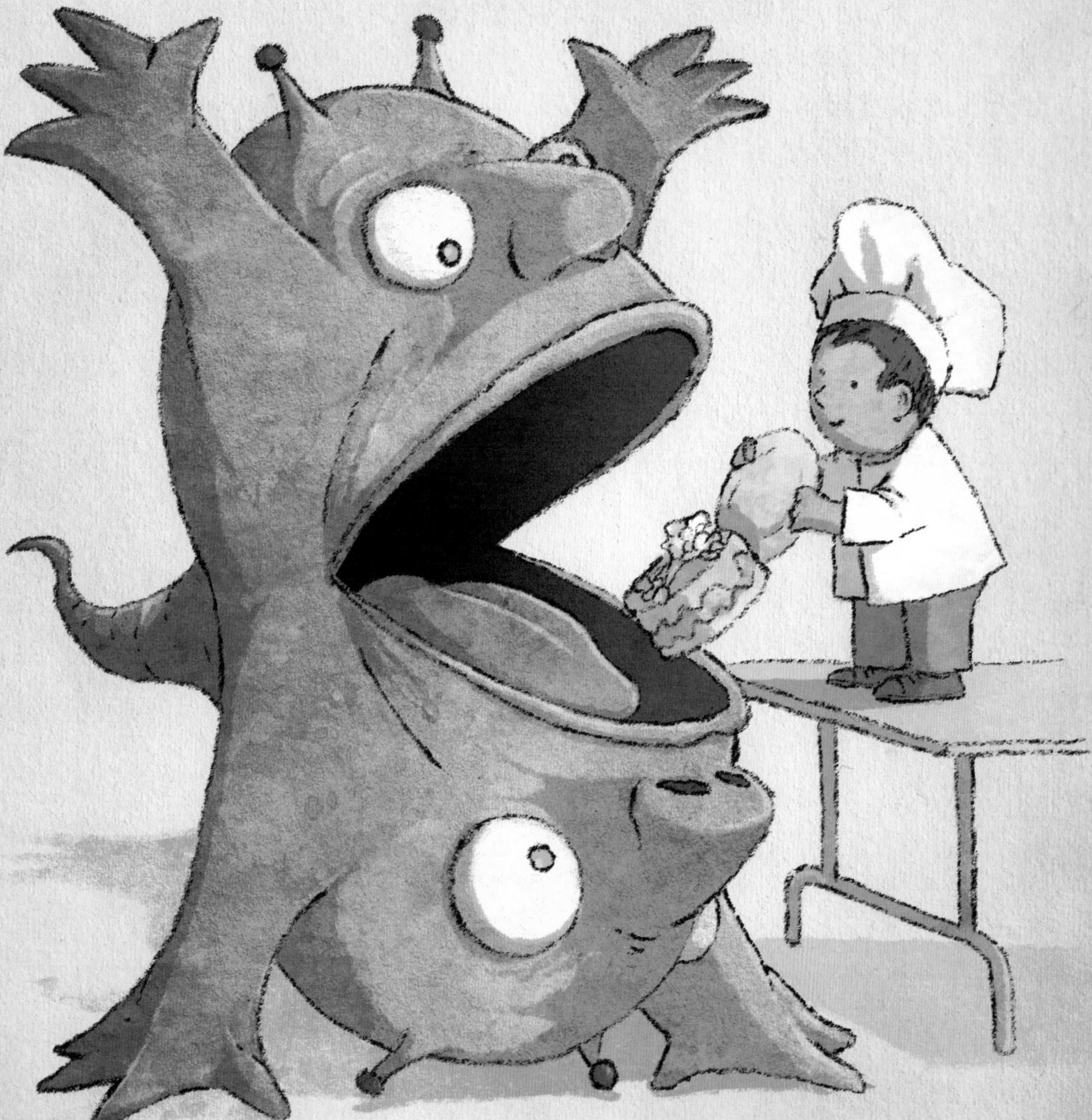

Some like my turnip-side-down cake.

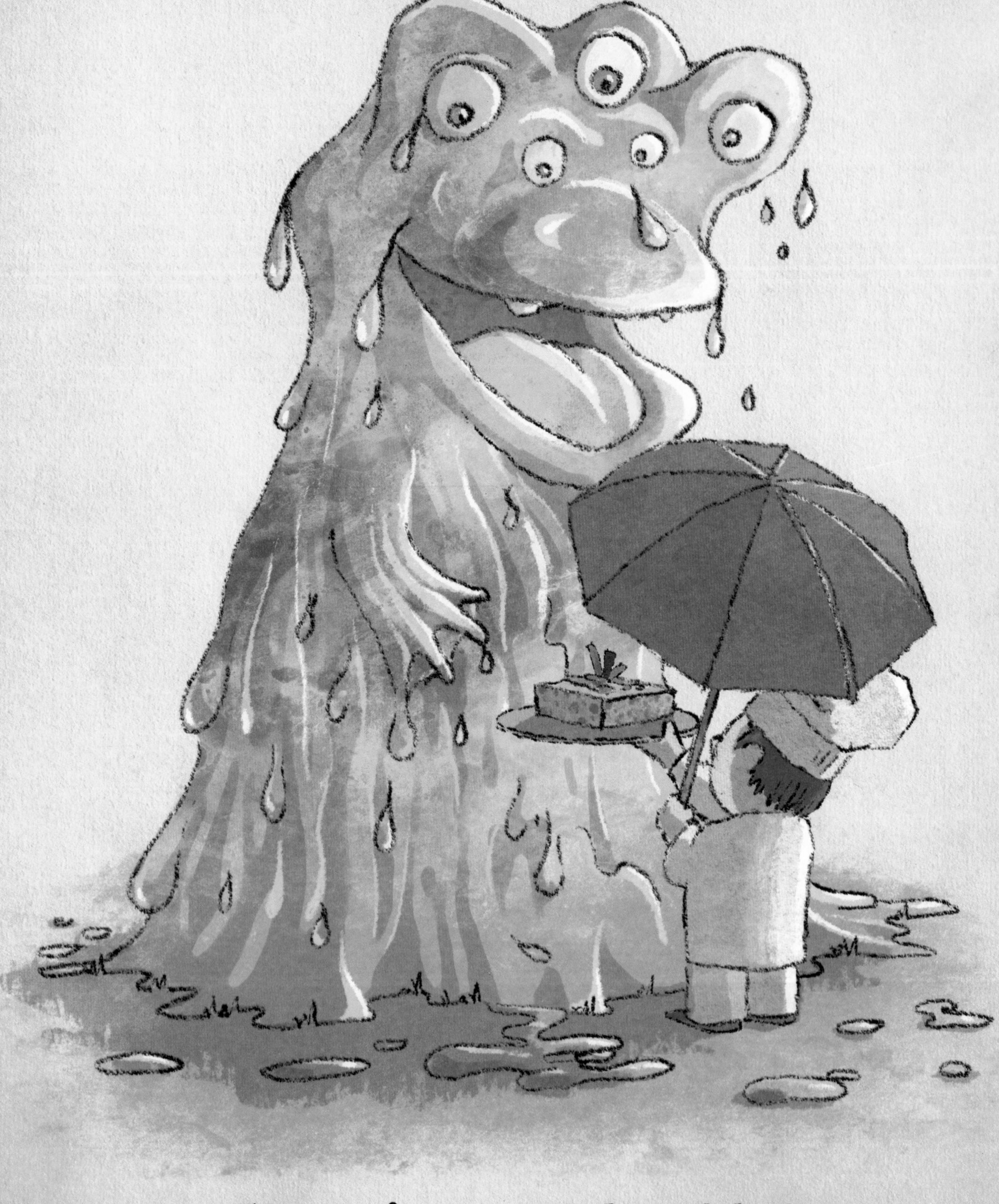

Some prefer sponge cake with leeks,

and bean puffs are especially popular
with the guys from the gas planets.

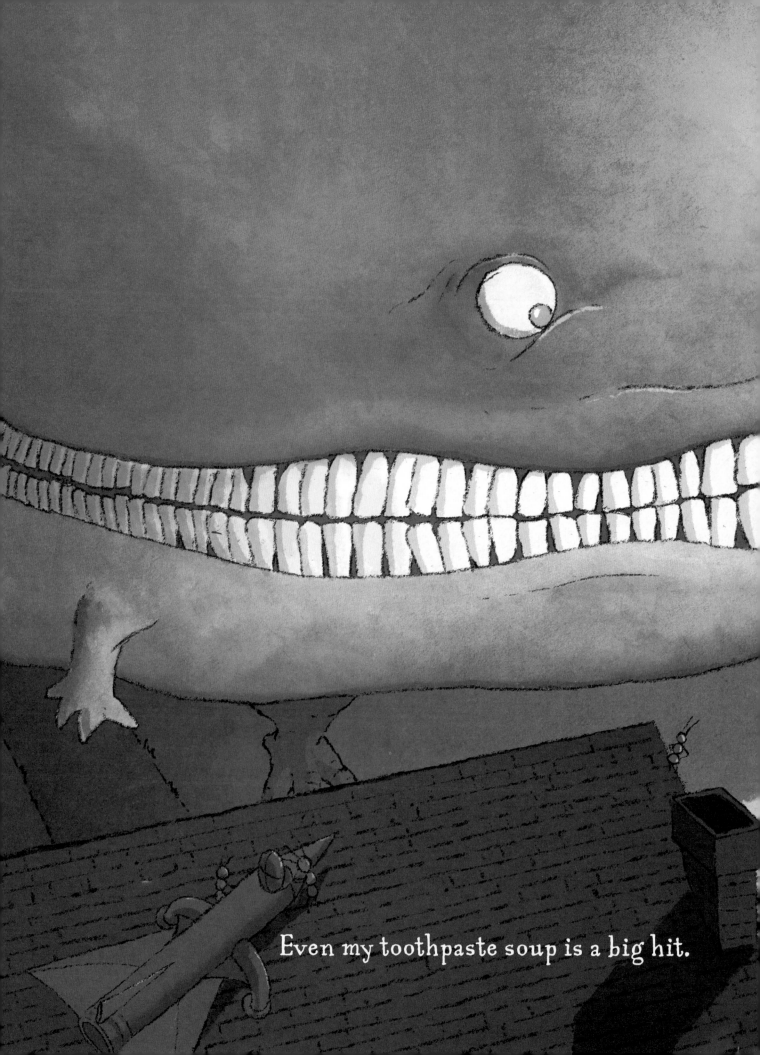

Even my toothpaste soup is a big hit.

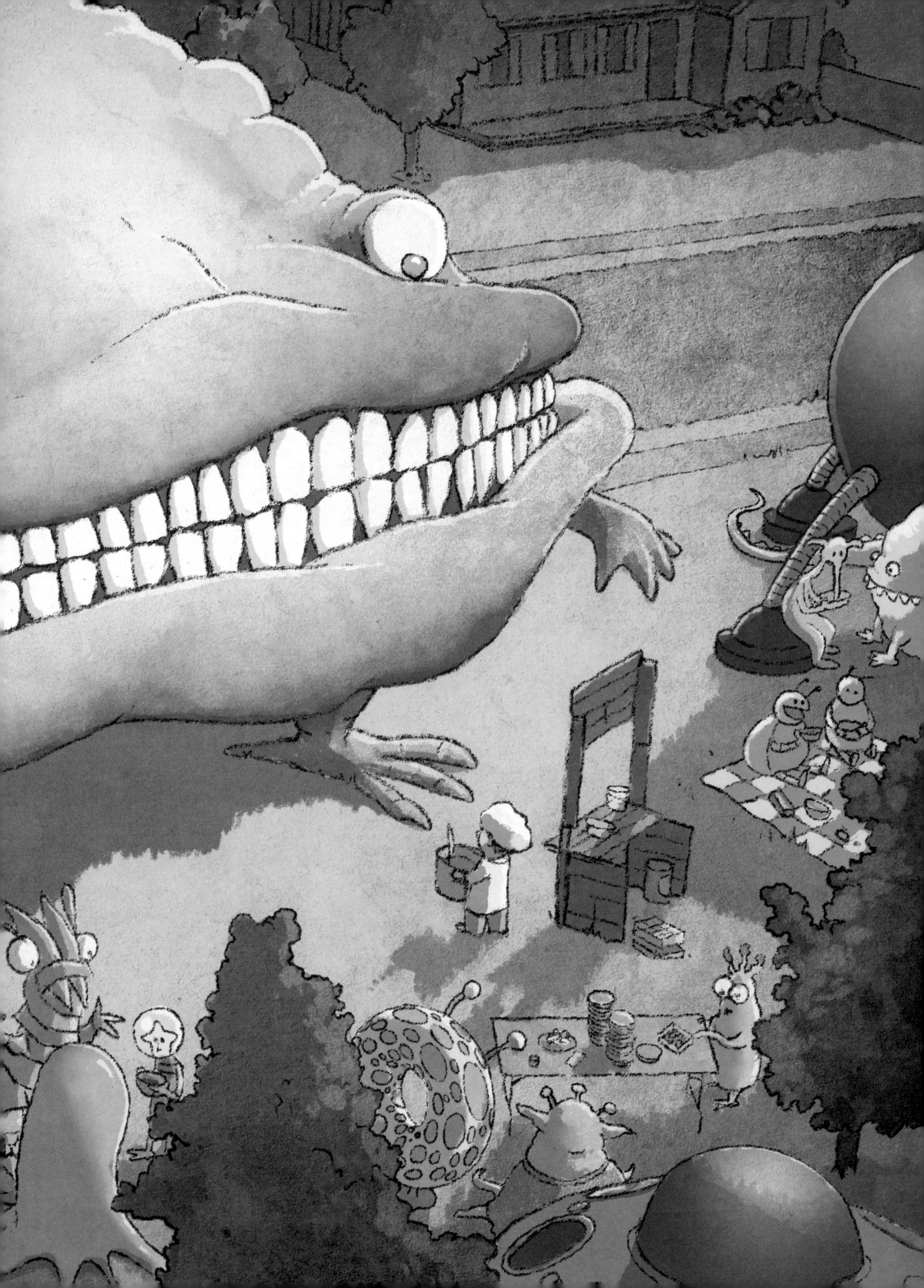

But next week, school starts. It's time to close up for the summer.

I decide to try something special for my last night: a dessert made from *every single one* of my favorite ingredients.

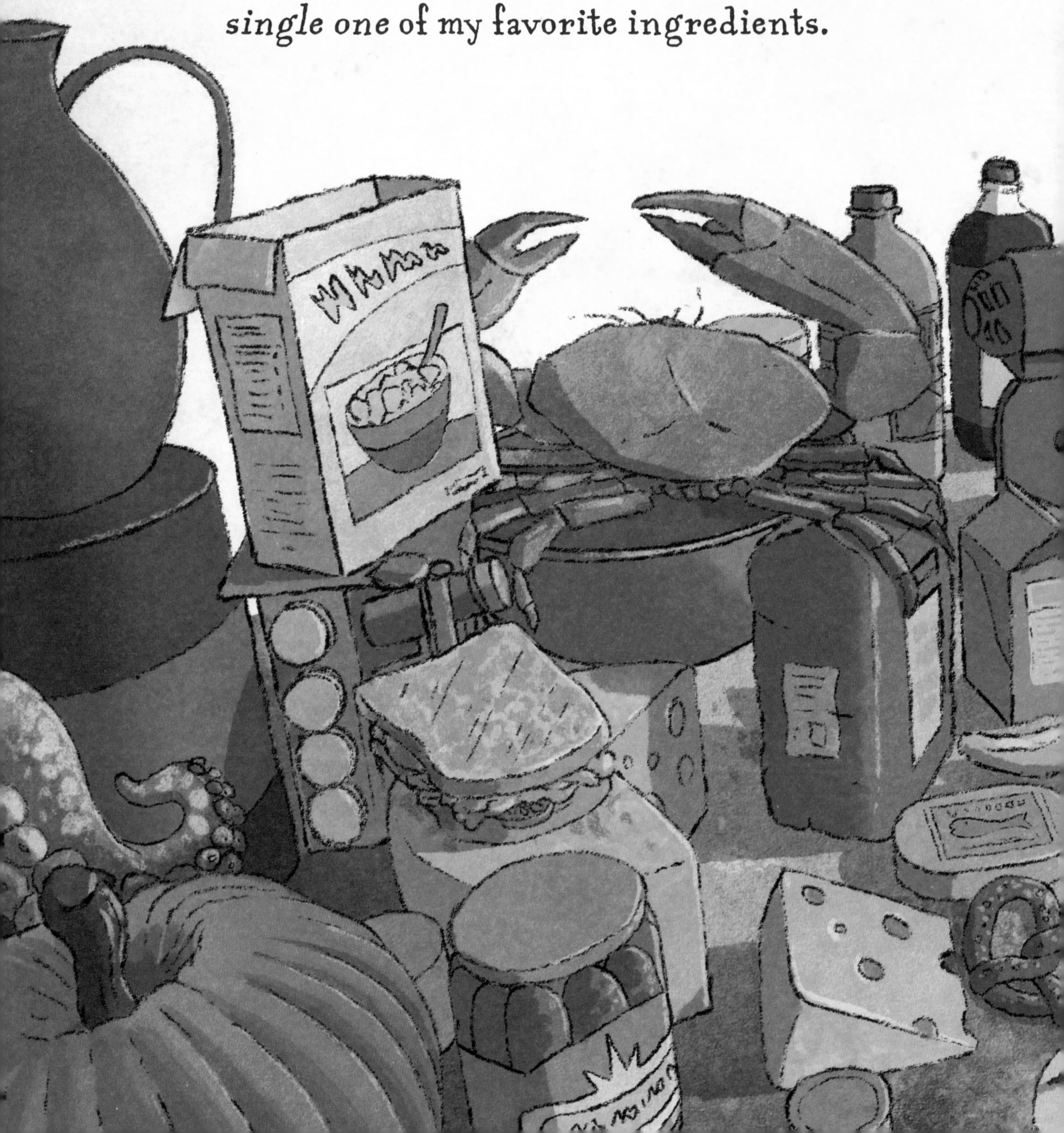

I call it Galactic
Pudding. It will be
my masterpiece.

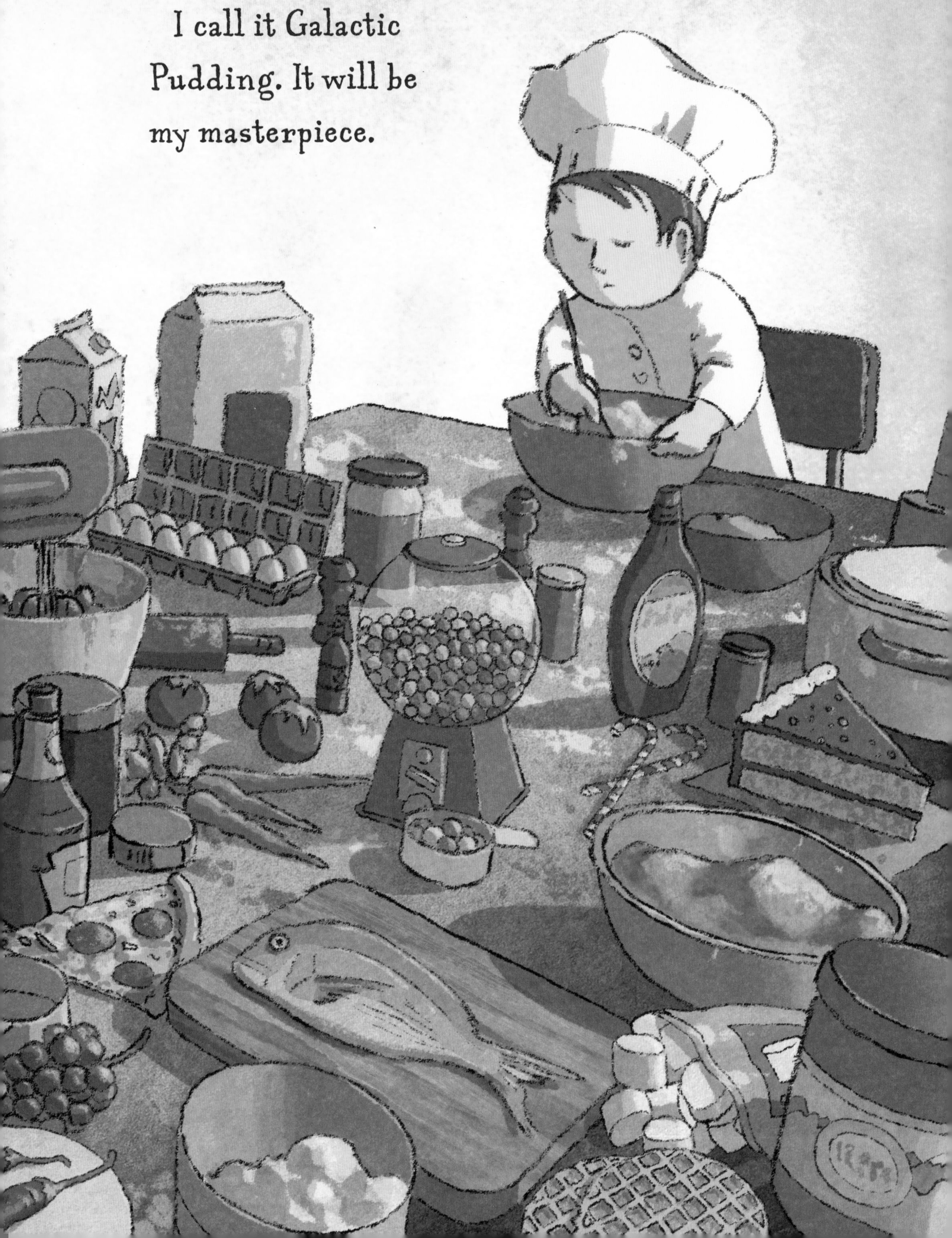

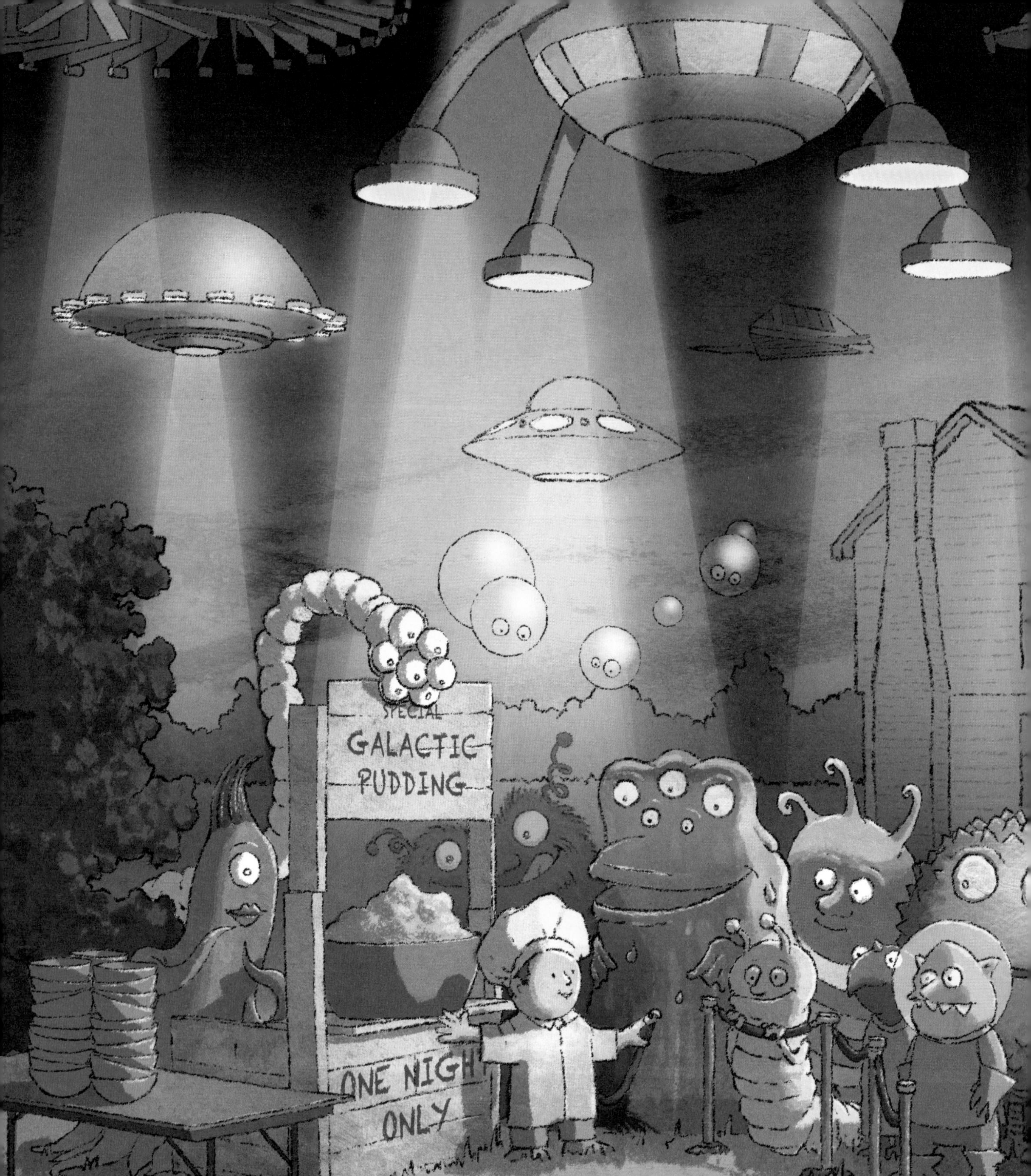
SPECIAL
GALACTIC
PUDDING
ONE NIGHT
ONLY

I open early. My customers are already lined up.

They can't wait to try the pudding...

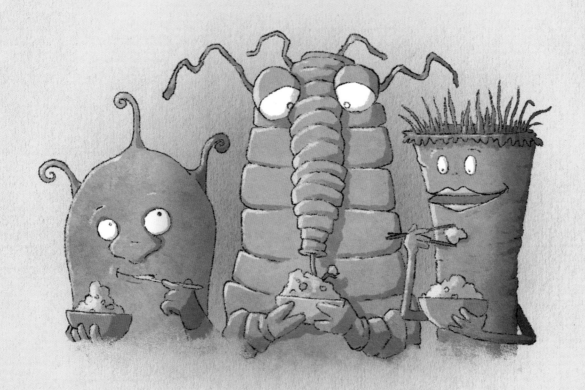

...and I can't wait to hear what
they think of it.

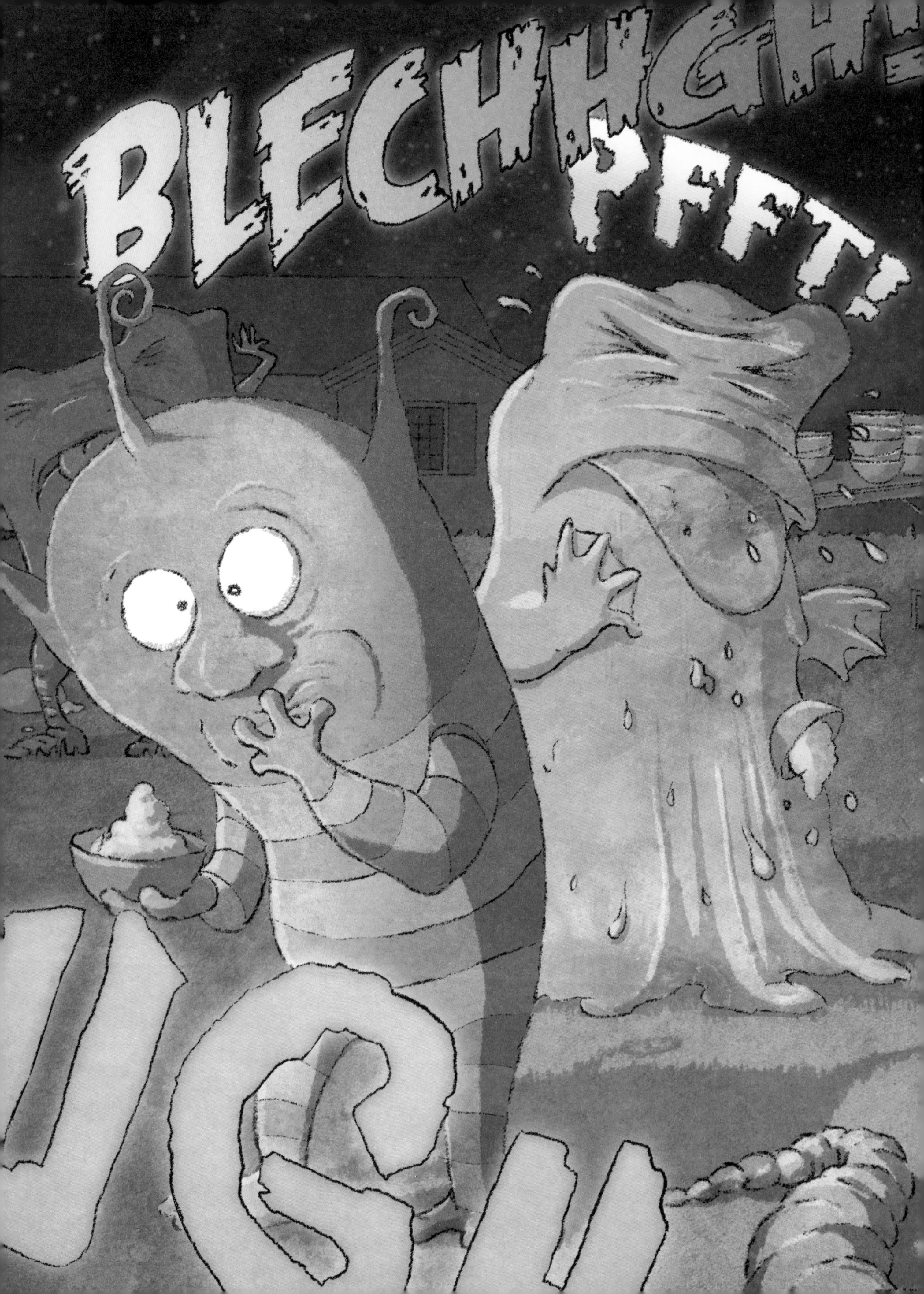
BLECHHGH!
PFFT!

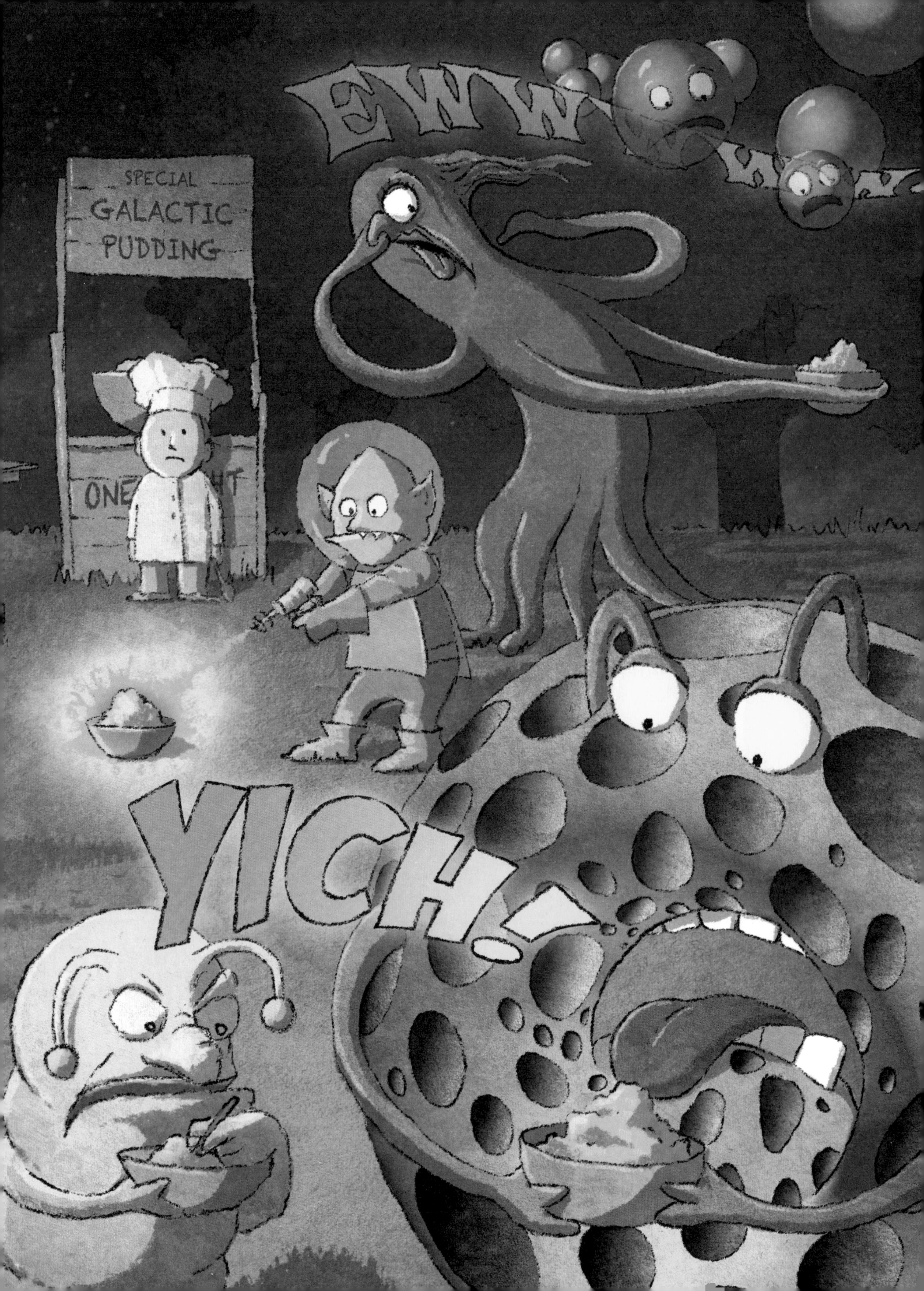
SPECIAL
GALACTIC
PUDDING
ONE
YICH!

Well, *I* liked it.

I guess my sister was right.

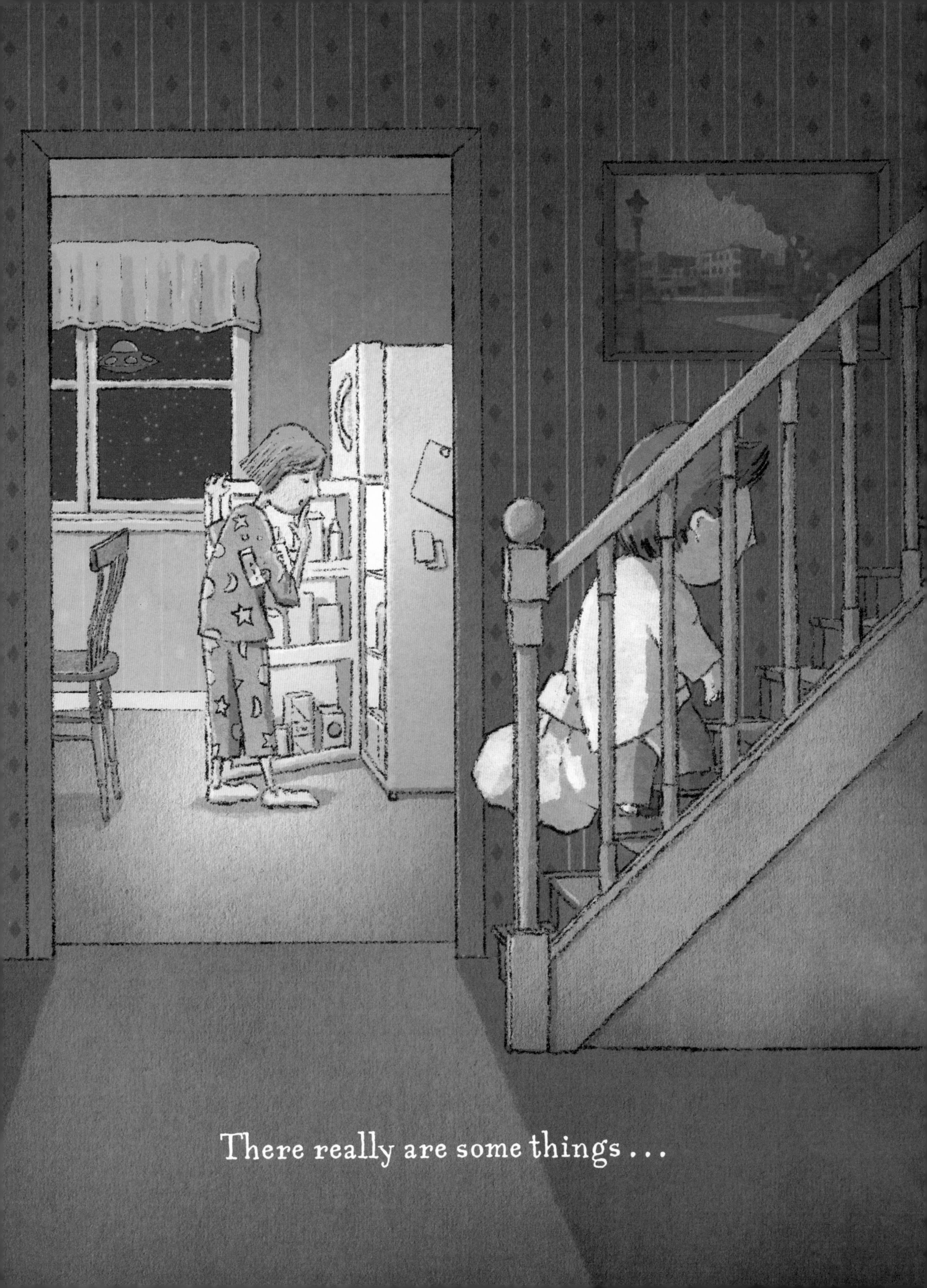

There really are some things . . .

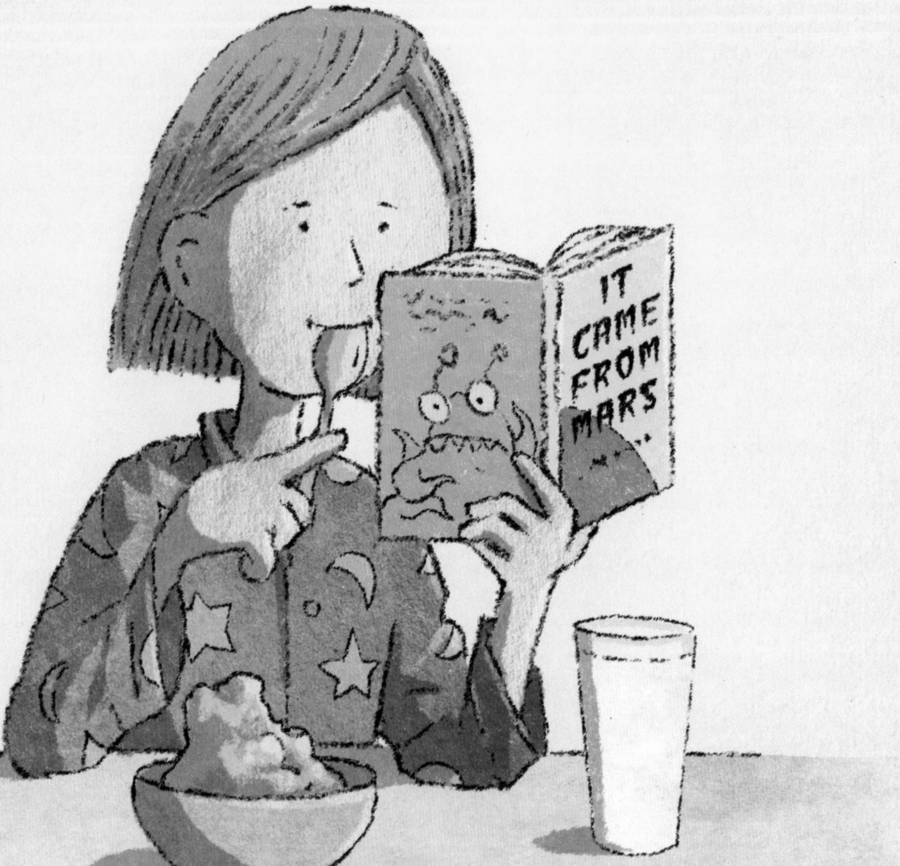
IT CAME FROM MARS

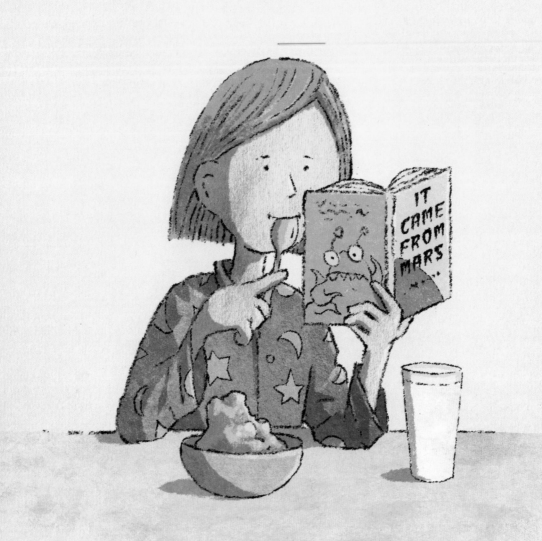

. . . no one else in the universe will eat.